D0935671

Watch Me

Watch Me

Norah McClintock

ORCA BOOK PUBLISHERS

Orca currents

Library and Archives Canada Cataloguing in Publication

McClintock, Norah

Watch me / written by Norah McClintock.

(Orca currents)

ISBN 978-1-55469-040-4 (bound).--ISBN 978-1-55469-039-8 (pbk.)

I. Title. II. Series.
PS8575.C62W38 2008   jC813'.54   C2008-903392-2

Summary: A battered watch might change Kaz's life.

First published in the United States, 2008
Library of Congress Control Number: 2008929298

Orca Book Publishers gratefully acknowledges the support for its publishing
programs provided by the following agencies: the Government of Canada
through the Book Publishing Industry Development Program and the
Canada Council for the Arts, and the Province of British Columbia
through the BC Arts Council and the Book Publishing Tax Credit.

Cover design by Teresa Bubela
Cover photography by Getty Images

Orca Book Publishers
PO Box 5626, Station B
Victoria, BC Canada
V8R 6S4

Orca Book Publishers
PO Box 468
Custer, WA USA
98240-0468

www.orcabook.com
Printed and bound in Canada.
Printed on 100% PCW recycled paper.

11 10 09 08 • 4 3 2 1

To the ones who are gone.

chapter one

I knew as soon as I saw the package that I wasn't getting what I wanted for my birthday.

"Well?" my mom said, beaming at me. "Aren't you going to open it?"

I ripped off the paper. I was right. It wasn't a games system. It was hockey equipment.

"Well, what do you say?" Neil said. Neil is my mom's boyfriend. He's an accountant, plus he coaches hockey. I hated that he lived with us.

"It's not what I asked for," I said.

The smile disappeared from my mom's face.

"But you used to love hockey," she said. "You used to play all the time."

"I used to play with Dad," I said.

My mom and dad split up a couple of years back, not long after I got out of the hospital. I saw my dad exactly twice after that. Then my mom got custody of me, and she wouldn't let me see him anymore. She blamed him for what had happened.

"Your mom put a lot of thought into that gift," Neil said. "I think you should apologize to her, Sport."

"I don't want to play hockey," I said. Phys ed was bad enough. There was no way I wanted to spend more time in a locker room with a bunch of guys who would only stare at me.

"But Evan said hockey would be good for you," my mom said. Evan was my social worker. "Team sports are a great way to make new friends. And you were good, Kaz. You could be the star of the team."

She just didn't get it.

"I'm not going to play hockey," I said. "I hate hockey."

I grabbed my jacket off a hook in the front hall and headed for the door.

"Where do you think you're going?" Neil said. "You are *not* leaving this house!"

"Oh yeah?" I said. "Watch me!"

I slammed the door behind me and stood on the porch for a moment, breathing hard. Neil must have decided to come after me because I heard my mom shout, "Neil, please! Leave him be."

Then I heard Neil say, "You can't let him get away with that type of behavior. It's time he learned—"

I ran down the front walk. I wanted to get as far from Neil as possible. I hated him.

Once I was outside, I pulled up the hood of my sweatshirt. I always wear it up when I'm not at school so that people can't stare at me. I'd wear my hood up at school too, if it wasn't against the rules. I hate being stared at.

I walked down the street as fast as I could. I hated my stupid so-called birthday present. I hated Neil and the way he called me Sport. I hated that my mom thought he was such a great guy. And I really hated that she had made my dad move out. That happened about a year after I saved my dad's life. He would have died, burned up in a fire, if it hadn't been for me. The whole thing was written up in the newspaper. It was on TV too. They said I was a hero. But being a hero isn't as great as you might think. For one thing, I was in the hospital for a long time and ended up with big ugly scars on one whole side of my body. The worst were the ones on the side of my neck and face. I missed a lot of school. When I finally went back, kids didn't treat me like a hero. They treated me like a freak because of all the scars. Plus I was way behind everyone else. I hate school. I hate phys-ed class. Sometimes I feel like I hate everything.

chapter two

"Neil's a jerk," Drew said the next day. "Forget about him."

"Easy for you to say," I said. "You don't have to see his ugly face everyday."

"True," Drew said. "Hey, I have to drop something off at my mom's work after school. You want to come?"

Drew's mom works at a bank on the other side of town. I didn't particularly want to go, but I had nothing better to do. Besides, Drew has been my best friend since he transferred to my school the year before last. He never makes fun of me. He never says anything about how I look—*ever*. He asked me about it one time, but he asked nicely, like he was just wondering, not like he thought I was some kind of freak. And when I answered, that was the last I heard of it. He never brought it up again. He never teases me about wearing my hood up all the time, and he doesn't try to pull it off me the way some guys do. As soon as school is over, and I pull up my hood, he puts on his baseball cap. He always grins at me when he does. It makes me feel like we're kind of the same, like we have our own way of doing things once the final bell rings. That's why I feel relaxed around him.

We rode the bus across town and then walked a couple of blocks to the bank.

"I'm not sure how long I'm going to be," Drew said. "It's old-lady day, so there might be a lineup."

"Old-lady day?"

Drew explained that a lot of seniors live in the neighborhood where his mom works.

Once a month, when their pension checks are deposited into their accounts, they trek to the bank to stand in line to take their money out.

"My mom says they don't like to use the instant teller," Drew said. "And a lot of them live alone. So they stand in line to take out their money and to talk to the teller. My mom says sometimes that's the only conversation they have all day."

It sounded pretty sad to me.

"I'll wait for you out here," I said.

Drew went inside. I hung out on the corner and watched one old lady after another come out of the bank. They all had grey hair and they all had purses hooked over their arms. Seven or eight of them came out while I waited for Drew. They all crossed at the light on the corner and walked toward the high-rise apartment buildings a few blocks away.

Finally Drew came out.

"You hungry?" he said.

I was always hungry. We picked up a couple of pizza slices. Drew said, "There's a park down that way. You want to hang out for a while, or do you have to go home right away?"

Neil usually gets home from work before my mom, so I was in no hurry.

"Let's go to the park," I said.

Another old lady came out of the bank while we waited for the light. She was wearing a black coat with a big pink flower pinned on it, and she was carrying a black purse. She was also wearing thick glasses. She walked down the street in front of us.

Drew finished his pizza slice and dug in his backpack for his Frisbee.

"Go out for a pass," he said.

The old lady was still ahead of us. She had already reached the park and was walking alongside it. I ran past her into the park. Drew's arm arced back and over his head. He sent the Frisbee sailing through the air. But it didn't come straight at me. Instead it curved to the left. I ran for it. I was in the clear too—until the old lady in the black coat suddenly started down the path that cut through the park. She must not have been paying attention. I yelled for her to look out, but all she did was turn and stare at me. Maybe she hadn't heard what I said. Then, *boink*, the Frisbee hit her on the side of the head. I saw the startled expression on her face. She staggered a little to one side. Her foot slipped off the path. Her ankle twisted. Then she crashed to the ground and just lay there.

I ran over to her.

"Are you okay?" I said.

Her glasses had fallen off, and her purse had slipped off her arm and was lying on the path. She reached out a hand so that I could help her up. And that's what I was going to do. I totally planned to help her. After that, I don't know what I was thinking.

No, that's not true. I do know.

I bent down to help her, and, all of a sudden, I thought about the stupid hockey equipment I got for my birthday because my mom and Neil thought it would be good for me. I thought about the games system I had asked for—and imagined Neil talking my mother out of it. I thought about my dad and how everything would be different if I lived with him instead of with my mom and Neil. I also thought about what Drew had said—that all those old ladies stood in line at the bank to take out money. Instead of helping the woman, I grabbed her purse.

Then I looked at Drew.

He stared at me like he wasn't sure what I was doing. He started toward me.

The old lady opened her eyes. She saw me with her purse in my hand. She tried to get up, but she couldn't. Drew was standing closest to her, and she grabbed him, startling him. He tried to shake her off, but she must have been stronger than she looked, because he had to really work at it. Finally, he shoved her. She fell backward onto the path. I heard a cracking sound and saw her head hit the cement. After that she didn't move.

I stared at her. Was she even breathing? I didn't know. I tucked the purse under my hoodie and ran.

chapter three

Someone grabbed my arm and yanked me to a halt.

Drew. He'd been pounding down the sidewalk behind me.

"There's a bus coming," he said, panting. He pointed up the street. We raced to the bus stop and got there just in time to jump on. Neither of us said a word all the way home. I didn't want to talk about what I'd done. I guess Drew didn't either. But as soon as we got off the bus, he grabbed

my arm again and dragged me into an alley
behind a bunch of stores and restaurants. After
checking to make sure that no one could see
us, he said, "So, let's see what you got."

By then I was shaking all over. I couldn't
believe what I'd done. If Neil had been
there, he would have been in the middle
of a big lecture about how I never thought
before I acted and how I got into trouble
because I let my temper take over.

Drew pulled the old lady's purse out of
my hands, took out the wallet and tossed
the purse back to me.

"Five bucks," he said after he pawed
through the wallet. "Check the purse, Kaz.
There's got to be more money in there."

There wasn't. There was just a bunch
of old lady stuff—lipstick, a little package
of tissues, a mirror and some powder, a
change purse filled mostly with pennies, an
empty glasses case—and a small box. Drew
snatched it and opened it.

"What is it?" I said.

"It looks like a watch," Drew said. He
lifted it out. It was old and rusted.

"Does it even work?" I said.

Drew held it up to his ear. He shook it. Finally, he turned it over and looked at the back. It was as rusted as the front, but I could make out some letters and numbers.

"It's junk," Drew said. "What a bust." He shook his head. "Make sure no one is watching us, Kaz."

I looked up and down the alley, but I didn't see anyone. Drew took all the ID out of the wallet. Most of it was plastic cards. He broke them into pieces. The rest was paper, which he ripped up. He walked down the alley and dropped all the pieces down a drain grate.

"What did you do that for?" I said.

"We don't want someone to find the wallet and connect it to that woman," Drew said. "We don't want the cops to know that we're not from her neighborhood."

He tossed the purse into a Dumpster.

"Let's get out of here," he said.

We walked to my street together. By then my legs were all wobbly. I kept thinking about that old lady and the noise her head had made when it hit the pavement.

"What if someone saw us?" I said.

"The cops have serious crimes to solve," Drew said. "Purse snatching isn't a big deal, especially this purse. It's not like there was thousands of dollars in there, Kaz. It's five bucks. The cops aren't going to put a bunch of ace detectives on the case. It'll probably take them a couple of hours to even show up. Maybe they won't even go to her place. Maybe they'll make her go down to the police station and file a report."

Maybe.

"She looked right at you, Drew."

"She's old," Drew said. "Her glasses came off. She probably just saw a big blur. Besides, we don't live anywhere near that neighborhood. I've only been over there once since my mom got transferred. No one knows us around there. If she tells the cops that some kids took her purse, they'll check out the local schools— assuming they check out anything at all. They'll never find you."

You. Because I was the one who'd taken the purse. Me—not Drew.

"You'll be fine, Kaz. Besides, you take stuff from stores all the time."

"I do not," I said. "Not *all the time.*" Sometimes I took stuff. Usually I did it when I was mad about something. It made me feel better. I don't know why. It just did.

"What I mean is, you've never been caught," Drew said. "Right?"

"Yeah, I guess." But that was different. Stores weren't old ladies. Nobody ever got hurt. "But—"

"It's kind of late to worry about it now," Drew said. "If you were going to get all nervous about it, you shouldn't have taken the purse in the first place."

He was right. It *was* too late to worry. What was done was done.

chapter four

Neil came through the front door at the same time he did every weekday. Usually he headed right into the kitchen. That was one of the things my mom liked about him. He didn't sit around waiting for her to show up. Instead he made supper. I was in the living room, watching TV. I slumped down on the couch, hoping he would walk right past me.

He didn't. He stopped, looked at me and said, "What are you up to, Sport?"

Was he blind? What did he think I was up to? I pretended I hadn't heard him.

He didn't go away. Instead he glanced at the TV.

"Watching the news?" he said. He sounded surprised. "You must really be bored. Why don't you get a start on your homework?"

That was typical Neil. No matter what I did, he had a problem with it. This was a perfect example. Neil liked to sit at the table at supper and talk about what was happening in the world—what wars were going on, what the politicians were doing, what the big issues in the city were. He usually gave me a hard time because I didn't care about stuff like that. So you'd think he would be happy that I was watching the news. But, no, he was making fun of me and telling me to do something else.

"This *is* homework," I lied. I hoped that would make him go away. It didn't. He stepped into the living room.

"You're doing current events in school now?" he said. "What's the focus? National? International?"

"My teacher wants us to see what's going on in the city," I said.

"And?"

"And what?"

"What's going on? What have you learned?"

So far, I'd learned that it looked like Drew was right. I had been flipping through all the local news stations, but I hadn't seen anything about the woman in the park. Not a thing.

The weather came on. I flipped off the TV, got up and brushed past Neil on my way to my room. He didn't try to stop me. I guess he thought I was going to do my homework.

If Neil hadn't already been reading the newspaper the next morning, I might have taken a look at it. Might have. But probably not. I don't like newspapers. I don't like magazines either. Or books. I don't like reading. It's too hard.

Neil glanced at me while I got myself some cereal. My mom was finishing a cup of coffee while she slid her feet into her shoes. She always leaves before Neil. She has to take two buses to get to the hospital where she's a lab technician. Neil can walk to work from our place. My mom pulled me toward her and kissed me on the cheek, which told me that she was in a good mood.

"All your homework done, Kaz?" she said.

I nodded. "Is it okay if I eat in the living room?" I said. "I have to watch the news."

She grinned. "Finally an assignment that's fun for you, huh?" she said. She knew how much I hated to read. She also knew how that made me feel about school.

Neil cleared his throat. My mom glanced at him before turning back to me.

"They're having sign-up for hockey at the arena tonight," she said. "If you want, we can go up there after supper and check it out."

That again.

"I already told you, I don't want to play hockey."

"But it would be fun," my mom said. "And maybe Drew would be interested. That way you'd already know someone—"

"No."

"Maybe you should give it a chance, Sport," Neil said. "Hockey would be good for you. When you're part of a team—"

"No!"

Neil stood up. He didn't like it when I yelled.

"It's okay," my mom said. She was smiling, but I could tell she was upset. "We don't have to talk about this now."

She kissed me on the cheek again. Then Neil walked her to the door. I heard them talking before she left, but I didn't care. I took my cereal into the living room, flopped down onto the couch and flipped on the TV. A few minutes later, the local news came on. There was still nothing about the old woman. What a relief.

I got through the morning and then caught up with Drew outside the cafeteria. He was dumping his lunch—a sandwich and an apple—into the garbage.

"Let's grab some pizza," he said.

I shook my head. "I don't have any money."

Drew checked the money in his pocket.

"I've got it covered," he said. "We'll go to the two-for-one place."

See what I mean about Drew? He never pressures me. He never gives me a hard time. Things are easy around him. He was the best friend a guy could have. We walked up the street to the pizza place and got a couple of slices. It was a nice day, so we walked around eating them. I had a good time. I didn't think about the old lady or her purse even once.

Then we went back to school and everything went wrong.

chapter five

It started with Rufus. It almost always started with him. He'd been giving me a hard time from the first day I met him.

After lunch on the second day of school, I'd found a note on my locker. It was on school letterhead, but the writing was all scribbley. I have a hard enough time reading without trying to figure out someone's crazy handwriting. But the note looked official, like it came from the office, so I tried.

Rufus's locker is right across from mine. He saw what I was doing and asked me if I needed help. I wanted to say no, but I also wanted to know what the note said. All I knew about Rufus at that point was that he was friends with a couple of the guys I used to go to elementary school with. But I didn't think he knew anything about me. And he sounded like he really wanted to help.

"Okay," I said finally.

Rufus took the note from me. "It's from Ms. Everett," he said. Ms. Everett is the principal at my school. "It says she wants you to come down to the office to discuss how come you're so stupid."

He said it as if he was reading it off the letter. I stared at him.

"I'm not kidding," he said. "That's really what it says." He was frowning, like he was as surprised as I was about what the note said. He glanced around and spotted one of his friends. "Hey, Tad! Come here."

Tad was standing a couple of lockers away with a few other guys. They all knew me from elementary school, and they all came down the hall toward us. Rufus handed him the note.

"What does this say?" he said.

Tad squinted at the note and then at me.

"It says that Catastrophe has to go to the office so that Ms. Everett can figure out why he's so stupid," he said. Tad had been calling me Catastrophe since fifth grade. I hated it. He handed the note to one of his friends. Before long, they had all read it, and they were all nodding and looking serious. Finally one of them burst out laughing. The next thing I knew, they were all laughing.

I grabbed the note from one of them, wadded it up and threw it into the garbage. My face was burning, and I knew it was bright red. That just made them laugh even harder. Drew fished the note out of the garbage can later when I told him what had happened.

"It's just scribbles," he said after he'd smoothed it out. "Rufus was just trying to get you going. He's a jerk."

Ever since then, I tried to stay out of Rufus's way, but it wasn't easy. He was always after me. He made me wish I was invisible. One of his favorite tricks was to sneak up behind me—in the schoolyard, in the hall, in the washroom, at the bus stop, anywhere he could find me—and pull my hood off. In class, where I wasn't allowed to have my hood up, he made a big deal of staring at my neck and the side of my face. In gym class, he liked to grab me and pull my T-shirt up so that everyone could see my side and my back. He got a big kick out of saying that he knew dogs that were smarter than me. He said even a stupid dog knew better than to run into a burning building instead of out of it.

The more I tried to dodge Rufus, the more he came after me. A person can only take so much—at least, this person can. So sometimes when he hassled me, it ended in a fight. I admit it: Most of the time when that happened, I was the one who threw the first punch. But that doesn't mean I was the one who started it. I never started anything. I never would have hit Rufus if he hadn't teased me or pulled down my hood or found a million ways to embarrass me. The thing is, he only ever did it when there were no teachers around. And whenever I lost my temper, he always got his friends to say that he hadn't done anything, that *I* had attacked *him*. That meant that I was the one who got in trouble. Always.

Like the day after I took that woman's purse.

Drew and I went back to school after lunch. I had a special reading period in the resource room with Ms. Larch, a teachers' aide. Halfway through, I glanced up and saw Rufus looking in through the window in the door. He was making faces at me. I tried to ignore him, but it was hard. Ms. Larch noticed that I wasn't paying attention. She glanced at the door. Rufus wasn't there anymore. A minute later, I took another look, and there he was again, grinning at me and making stupid faces. That went on for maybe ten minutes. But when the bell rang and I went out into the hall, he was gone. At least, that's what I thought. I started down the hall to my locker. All of a sudden, I tripped over something and landed face-first on the floor. My books and my binder went flying. Behind me, kids laughed. When I twisted my head around to see what I had tripped on, there was Rufus standing in the doorway to a classroom. I wasn't one hundred percent positive, but I was willing to bet anything—anything at all—that he had tripped me on purpose. Everything in front of my eyes turned red and then black. I flew at Rufus and caught him right at the knees. He crashed to the floor. Everything went quiet in the hall. Then I hit him.

I hit him just as Ms. Larch came out of the resource room. She saw the whole thing. At least, she thought she did. She saw me fly at Rufus and hit him. She didn't see what had happened before, and, for sure, none of Rufus's friends were going to tell her. Ms. Larch told me to get up. A girl—Jana King—picked up my binder. A bunch of the pages had fallen out. She picked them up too, and stood there staring at them and frowning. Great, someone else was taking a good long look at how stupid I was. I grabbed the binder and the papers out of her hand. Ms. Larch saw me do that too.

"Jana is just trying to help," she said. She told me to apologize to her. But by then, the vice-principal had turned up. He talked to Ms. Larch and then walked me down to the office.

Ms. Everett looked disappointed but not surprised to see me. She shook her head, gave me a detention and told me that she was going to have to call my mom. She asked me if I had anything to say for myself.

I did. "Please don't call her," I said. My mom would freak if she heard I'd been tagged for fighting again. Neil would be even worse. He'd lecture me all night.

"I'm sorry, Kaz," Ms. Everett said. "But you know the rules. You're lucky I don't suspend you."

I didn't feel lucky.

chapter six

That afternoon, instead of going home like everyone else, I went to detention. Two other kids had detention that day: Jonathan Morris and—big surprise—Jana King.

"What's *she* doing here?" I asked Jonathan.

"I heard she slapped some girl," Jonathan said. "People think girls are sweet, but when they get mad, look out."

"What was she mad about?"

Jonathan just shrugged. "Probably girl stuff," he said. "You should have seen her in the office after. She was crying and begging Ms. Everett not to call her parents. She promised she'd do anything if Ms. Everett didn't call." He shook his head in disgust.

I stared at Jana as she took a seat at the back of the room. She was smart and popular—she was always on the honor roll, and she had a million friends. Drew called her The Princess behind her back, partly because her last name was King and her family lived in a big house on Royal Avenue, and partly because she seemed so perfect. It was hard to imagine her hitting anyone. But Jonathan was right. You never know about girls. Just because they look sweet, doesn't mean they act sweet all the time. To be honest, I wanted to laugh knowing that Jana King was in detention for more or less the same reason that I was.

Mr. Porelli, who was in charge of detentions that day, made all three of us move up to the front of the room where he could keep an eye on what we were doing.

"I'm going to give you a break, people," he said. "I'm going to let you get a head start on your homework."

This was supposed to be a big deal, because a lot of teachers who were in charge of detention made you write an essay about whatever stupid thing had landed you there and what you could have done differently. I hate writing stuff like that—I hate writing anything—mostly because my spelling is pretty bad. So is my handwriting. So I guess it was nice that Mr. Porelli wasn't making us write anything. But doing homework is just as hard for me as writing an essay, so it wasn't like he was doing me a huge favor.

I pulled out my math book and opened it. I did the first part of my math homework okay—it was equations, you know, solving for x. I'm not so bad at that. But the second part was harder. My math teacher had assigned ten word problems. The first one went: *John is building a fence around his mother's garden, which is shaped like an isosceles trapezoid with a square attached to the shortest end. If the sides of the trapezoid section are 200 m, 500 m and 800 m, and the side length of the square is 200 m, how much fencing does John need?* You can't believe how much trouble I had just reading and figuring out the questions, never mind trying to find the answer. The more words in the question, the harder it was for me to work out what I was supposed to do. I puzzled over that first question for at least five minutes. Mr. Porelli glanced at me a couple of times, but he didn't say anything. I could have asked him for help, but I didn't know him very well and I didn't know what he knew about me. I don't like asking people who don't know about me. I don't even like asking people who do know, but at least then I don't have to explain why I'm having trouble.

Mr. Porelli got up. He said, "I'm going to trust you people to behave yourselves and do your work while I'm out of the room for a few minutes. Don't disappoint me."

He didn't have to worry about me. Things were bad enough. If I got into trouble while I was already in detention, I don't know what my mom would have done. So I kept my eyes on my work. But Jana didn't keep her eyes on hers.

"That's not right," she said.

At first I didn't think she was talking to me. She had never talked to me before. But when I glanced up, I saw that she was looking at my math binder.

"You're doing that all wrong," she said.

"Who asked you?" I said. I hate when people look at what I'm doing. I hate it even more when they tell me I'm wrong—like I don't know that already.

"You're supposed to add five hundred plus eight hundred plus two hundred times four," she said.

I stared at her. What was she even talking about? I turned back to my work and pretended I hadn't heard what she had said.

"Fine," she said. "If you want to get it wrong, be my guest."

"Why don't you just mind your own business?" I said.

"I know how to do math," she said. "I *tutor* math."

"Big deal," I said. I turned sideways in my seat and put my arm alongside my work so that she wouldn't be able to look at it. I think she was going to say something else to me, but Mr. Porelli came back into the room. That shut her up.

By the time Mr. Porelli let us go, the school was almost deserted. I went to my locker and got what I needed for the night. Then I headed for the door. On the way down the stairs, I ran into Jana. I didn't want to talk to her, but she stepped right in front of me.

"I wasn't trying to tell you what to do or anything," she said. "It's just that I've heard about you and—"

She'd *heard* about me?

"You heard how stupid *I* am so you thought you'd tell me how smart *you* are, is that it?" I said. "Okay, so now I know. But let me ask you something—do your parents know that their little princess goes around hitting girls? Or did turning on the waterworks convince Ms. Everett to make an exception for you and not call them?"

Jana stared at me. Her face turned red. Her lips started to tremble. Her eyes got all watery—what a baby!—and she wiped at them with the back of her hand.

"What I meant was, I saw some of the papers that fell out of your binder earlier," she said. "You mix up a lot of letters. You're dyslexic, right?"

I felt my hands turn into fists. I hate that word. I hate when people say it.

"I have a cousin who has the same problem," she said. "He's good at math, like you, except when they're word problems. Then he has trouble. I was going to ask if you had tried the peer-tutoring program, because I tutor my cousin sometimes, and he says it helps. But forget it, okay?"

She spun around and started down the stairs. She was moving fast, even though she wasn't supposed to be running on the stairs. Her dark brown hair flew out behind her.

I watched her for a moment, and then I chased after her. I didn't catch up to her until she had reached the main doors.

"I'm sorry," I said. Punching Rufus was one thing. Making a girl cry, especially when it turned out that she wasn't trying to give me a hard time after all—that was something else. "Really, I'm sorry."

When she turned and looked at me, I saw that she'd been crying again. She didn't say a word. She just raced out of the school. I felt like an idiot for apologizing. It never got me anywhere.

chapter seven

Neil was making supper when I got home. I could tell from the way he popped his head out of the kitchen to look at me that Ms. Everett had called my mom, and my mom had called Neil. But he didn't say anything. He never did. He always waited for my mom.

My mom got home an hour after I did. I was in my room, but I heard her come through the door. I heard her drop her purse on the floor beside the table in the front hall. I heard her talking to Neil, but I couldn't make out what they were saying. For the longest time after Neil moved in, I thought my mom agreed with him about everything. I never heard them fight. But after a while that started to change. They started to close the door of whatever room they were in, and I would hear from the sharpness in their voices that they were arguing. This was one of those times.

Finally someone knocked on my door.

"Who is it?" I called.

"It's me."

My mom. I told her to come in.

But when she opened the door, I saw that Neil was with her. They stood side by side at the foot of my bed.

"Ms. Everett called me at work," my mom said.

"It wasn't my fault."

My mom shook her head. She looked tired. She glanced at Neil.

"Ms. Larch saw what happened," he said.

"No, she didn't. She only saw part of it."

"But you did knock that boy to the ground, didn't you, Sport?"

"Yeah, but that's because—"

Neil cut me off. "And you hit him, didn't you?" he said.

"He deserved it," I said. "He—"

My mom sat down on the edge of my bed.

"Oh, Kaz," she said.

"But, Mom, you don't understand—"

"There's no excuse for fighting, Kaz." She sounded as tired as she looked. Worse, she sounded disappointed. "You used to be so happy. You never made any trouble. You never got into fights. You were always outside with your hockey stick playing road hockey, ice hockey..." Her eyes glistened with tears. Geez, was everyone going to cry today? "Remember, Kaz? Remember that boy?"

Neil came up behind her and squeezed her shoulder.

"I think what your mother is trying to say, Sport, is—"

"I want to live with Dad," I said.

That took my mom by surprise.

"What?" she said.

"I want to live with Dad."

I thought about the old lady and her purse. I wished it had had lots of money in it. If it had, I would have used it to buy a bus ticket. I would have gone to my dad's place.

"Your dad has a new family now," my mom reminded me, as if that were something I could ever forget. I'd been stunned when she told me. She hadn't seemed happy about it either. A few weeks ago, I heard her complain to Neil that having a new baby was my dad's latest excuse for not sending child support payments like he was supposed to. She said she hadn't got a check from him in over three months. But I didn't care about that.

"He's still my dad. I can be with him if I want to."

"But you haven't seen him in years," my mom said.

"Whose fault is that?"

"Watch the tone, Sport," Neil said. He still had his hand on my mom's shoulder.

"You think *I'm* to blame?" Mom said.

"He's the one who decided to move so far away."

"He moved after you wouldn't let him have joint custody," I said. "You never let him see me."

"It's more complicated than that," my mom said slowly. "Your dad..." She shook her head. "It's just complicated, Kaz. And now that you have a little sister..." There were more tears in her eyes now. "We can talk about this another time. For right now, you need to know that what you did today was wrong. I know you're having a hard time in school. But you can't take your frustration out on other kids. It's not right. I know you're a better person than that. I just know it." She stood up. "Supper will be ready in half an hour."

"I'm not hungry."

Half an hour later when she called me to come and eat, I didn't answer. She didn't call again. I heard dishes clinking in the kitchen. I smelled food—I think it was Neil's meatloaf. I didn't like Neil, but he made good meatloaf. My stomach rumbled. My mouth watered. But I stayed in my room until the next morning after both Neil and my mom had gone to work.

My mom had left my lunch on the kitchen table in a brown paper bag. I peeked inside. It was a thick meatloaf sandwich. It looked so good that I ate it for breakfast. It put me in a good mood—until I got to school and found Jana waiting at my locker.

"I just wanted to say I'm sorry about yesterday," she said.

She was sorry? I was the one who had been mean to her. Why was she apologizing?

"I guess I did sort of come across like some kind of know-it-all," she said. "And then I got all emotional. I hate that. I hate when I cry in front of people. Especially people I don't know very well."

She meant people like me.

"I was embarrassed," she said. "I mean, I *never* hit people. Never."

Unlike me.

"And then..." Her cheeks turned pink. "Do you know Alicia Seretta?"

I nodded.

"Well, she said something stupid. Normally I would have ignored her. I guess I should have. But I didn't."

"What did she say?"

Jana studied me for a minute, like she was trying to decide if I was really interested. Or maybe she was trying to decide if she wanted to stand there and talk to me when she could have been hanging out with her millions of friends.

"Alicia did some community service at a seniors' center," she said finally. "She was telling everyone how much she hated it. She said old people were a waste of space. We got in an argument and..." She shook her head. "I've never slapped anyone before. But she wouldn't stop. It's like she thinks if you're old, you're useless, and, well, I guess it got to me because my grandma is in the hospital."

Oh.

"I'm sorry," I said. "Is she sick?"

"Someone pushed her down and stole her purse," she said. "She hit her head really hard. She's seventy-five years old." Her eyes started to fill up with tears again. She wiped at them with the back of her hand. "Here I go again," she said. "I'm sorry about yesterday. I just wanted to tell you that. And if you ever need help with math or anything, you can ask me."

She turned then and ran down the hall to the girls' bathroom. I watched the door close behind her. I wondered where her grandma lived. I wondered what the chances were.

chapter eight

No way, I told myself. It's a big city. It was just a weird coincidence that someone had stolen Jana's grandma's purse.

But I couldn't stop thinking about it.

I watched for Jana in the hall that afternoon, but I didn't see her anywhere. So at the end of the day, I went up to a girl who I knew was a friend of Jana's and I asked her where Jana's locker was. The girl looked at me like I was crazy—like, why was a guy like me even thinking about Jana, let alone looking for her locker? She told me, but the way she said it, she made it sound like it was a waste of her breath and would be a waste of my time to go to Jana's locker. I told myself that I should forget it. I didn't want to run into that girl again. But I had to find out.

I headed down the hall the girl had told me. Sure enough, there was Jana. There were some other kids in the hall too, taking stuff out of their lockers and putting stuff in. But none of them were anywhere near Jana. I took a deep breath and started toward her.

Jana didn't notice me at first. She was busy putting books into her backpack. I wasn't sure what to say, so I just stood there and watched her. She jumped when she finally turned around and saw me.

"Hey, Kaz," she said. That surprised me. My school is big, but it's not that big, so I guess it didn't mean anything that she knew my name. But I had never heard her say it before. There was something about a girl like Jana knowing my name and saying it that made me feel good.

"I was thinking about what you said about your grandmother," I said.

Her cheeks turned pink.

"I'm sorry," she said. "I told you I didn't like to cry in front of people, and then I burst into tears all over again."

"You don't have to keep apologizing," I said. "When people are sad, they cry." My mom sure did. "It's natural. Anyway, I was wondering about your grandmother. Is she going to be okay?"

"She didn't break anything when she fell," Jana said. Anger flashed in her eyes. "I mean, when she got knocked down. But she hit her head on the sidewalk, so they're keeping her in the hospital for observation. They want to make sure that there's no permanent damage."

"Did she see who did it?" I hoped it sounded like a normal question that anyone might ask.

"I'm not sure," Jana said. "We went to the hospital to see her, but she was sleeping. The nurse said she seemed disoriented." Her lower lip started to tremble. "That could mean some kind of brain damage. Or it could just be something temporary. We don't know yet. I'm going to see her again today. I hope she's okay. And I hope she saw who did it and that the police catch the person. It's bad enough stealing from her. But knocking down an old person like that? You could kill them."

I felt sick inside. If it *was* a coincidence, it was the world's biggest one.

"Did she have a lot of valuable stuff in her purse?"

"She told one of the paramedics that she didn't have much money in her wallet," Jana said.

I felt even sicker. There hadn't been much money in the purse I had taken.

"But all her ID was in there, and it's going to be a hassle to replace. The thing that's really horrible, though, is the watch."

I thought about the little box that Drew had found inside the purse I had taken.

"She talked to my dad just before she left her apartment that day. She had a watch in her purse—a watch that she was going to send to my brother."

"But it's—" I stopped myself just in time. I had been going to say that the watch was rusted and didn't even work.

Jana frowned at me. "It's what?"

"Nothing," I said. "Can't she just buy another watch?"

Jana shook her head.

"This watch is special. It belonged to my grandma's older brother. He was a pilot during World War Two. His plane was shot down over the jungle in Burma. You know where that is?"

I nodded, even though I was pretty sure I'd never even heard of a place called Burma.

"My grandma says she can still remember the day they sent someone to her house. She says it was the minister of her parents' church. He came to tell them that her brother was missing."

"Missing? So he didn't die when his plane was shot down?"

"That's the thing," Jana said. "Grandma always says that was the worst part. They just said he was missing, so for the longest time, my grandma and her parents and her brothers and sister kept hoping that he would turn up. They thought that maybe he'd been captured and was in a prisoner-of-war camp somewhere. They contacted the Red Cross to see if they could find out where he was."

"And did they?"

She shook her head.

"After the war ended and they hadn't found out anything, they figured that he must have died—maybe when his plane was shot down, or maybe after, you know, in the jungle. Or maybe he had been in a prisoner-of-war camp and had died there. But they never knew for sure what happened to him. My grandma says it was horrible. She says that even though her parents knew he must be dead, they always hoped he would show up one day."

"But he never did, huh?"

"No."

"So, this watch your grandma had— did her brother give it to her before he went away?"

Jana shook her head again.

"He had it with him when he left for overseas. He had it when he was shot down."

"I don't get it," I said. "I thought you said they never found him."

"They didn't. But a couple of years ago, a hunter found this old rusted watch in the jungle in Burma. He showed it to some missionaries. They saw the engraving on the back of it and realized that it had belonged to someone who had been in the air force. It had a name and a serial number on it. They sent it to Veterans Affairs, and they tracked down my grandmother. They returned the watch to her a month ago. They say they're going to organize a search to see if they can find my great-uncle and the rest of the people who were in the plane so that they can be buried here at home."

I stared at her.

"You're kidding, right? I mean, that watch must have been there for"—I tried to do the math in my head—"more than sixty years."

"Sixty-five years," she said.

I felt terrible. That watch had been in the jungle since way before my parents were born. Then someone had found it and had traced it back to Jana's grandmother. Now I had ruined everything.

"My great-uncle was twenty-five when he died," Jana said. "That's why my grandma wanted my brother to have his watch."

I didn't get it.

"What's why?" I said.

"My brother is in the armed forces. He turned twenty-five this year. He's in Afghanistan right now. My grandma was on her way to a watch repair place to see if they could clean it up and get it working again."

Oh.

"My dad says my grandma probably doesn't care about anything else that was in that purse. But she does care about the watch," Jana said. "He also says that whoever took her purse probably thought the watch was just a piece of junk and probably tossed it into the garbage." I felt my cheeks get hot. "He says she'll never see the watch again, but he hasn't told her that yet. He doesn't want to say anything until he knows for sure the police can't find it or at least find out who stole her purse. He also wants to make sure she's going to be okay before he gives her the bad news." Her eyes started to fill with tears again, which made me feel even worse.

"I wish there was some way I could help," I said.

"It's nice of you to say that, Kaz," she said, wiping away her tears. "But what could you possibly do?"

It was a good question.

"I have to go," she said. "I want to see how my grandma is. Have a good weekend."

"You too," I said.

chapter nine

I was supposed to go straight home after school, but I didn't. Instead I went back to the alley where Drew and I had ditched the purse. The Dumpster was still there. Or, at least, *a* Dumpster was there. I couldn't tell if it was the same one. I also couldn't tell if it had been emptied or not. To find out, I had to drag some crates over and stack them up so that I could climb on top and look inside. The garbage came three-quarters of the way to the top. I didn't see the purse, but if this was the same Dumpster, a lot of other stuff must have been thrown into it in the past three days.

I looked around but didn't see anyone. There were eight or nine doors that opened into the alley, but no windows. I was in the clear.

I took another look into the Dumpster. There were a lot of green garbage bags in it, but there was no bad smell. I also saw scraps of foam rubber, big chunks of Styrofoam, a broken chair and a big tangle of wire. I didn't see anything that looked like rotten food or, worse, anything moving, like, say, rats.

I hauled myself up until I got one leg over the edge of the Dumpster. Then I pulled my other leg up and sat on the edge with my legs dangling down inside. I looked at all the garbage. Maybe the purse was in there, and maybe it wasn't. There was only one way to find out for sure. I took a deep breath and dropped down into the Dumpster.

One of my feet landed on a green garbage bag and broke it. Something leaked all over

my sneaker and soaked into my sock. I
pulled my foot out. It was covered in goo.
At first I thought, what *is* that? What if it's
poison? What if it eats into my foot? What
if—? I almost gave up right then. Then I
thought about what Jana had told me, and
I put my foot down onto another spot.

I wished I had a pair of gloves, but it
was too late to do anything about that.
Carefully, in case something sharp was
hiding under all the garbage, I began to
hunt through the Dumpster. At first I piled
stuff on one side as I dug down. But when
the pile got too high, things began to fall
back onto me. So then I started throwing
stuff out into the alley. That made it a little
easier. I dug and dug. Pretty soon it started
to smell. The green garbage bags that were
near the bottom were all broken, and there
was more goo—smelly goo—all over the
place. I tried to breathe through my mouth
as I continued searching.

Finally I made it to the metal floor of
the Dumpster. The smell was making me
gag. I had thrown a lot of stuff out and

was down so deep that I started to worry I wouldn't be able to climb out again.

That's when I spotted it.

The purse.

I would have recognized it anywhere.

I opened it.

All the stuff that had been in there when Drew looked through it was still there—except for the ID that Drew had destroyed, and the watch. Maybe it had fallen out.

I looked everywhere, but I couldn't find it.

Something wet fell on me.

Then something else.

It had started to rain.

I looped the purse strap over my arm and jumped up to grab the edge of the Dumpster.

I missed.

I jumped again—and missed again.

I started to panic. What if I was trapped in here?

I took a deep breath and jumped a third time. This time I caught hold of the edge and held tight. Finally I got one leg over and then the other. I dropped down into the alley.

More than half the stuff that had been in the Dumpster was now spread all over the alley. I thought about putting it all back, but the rain was coming down hard. One of the doors into the alley opened and a man stepped out. He looked at all the garbage. Then he spotted me.

"Hey," he yelled. "What do you think you're doing?" He started toward me, like he was going to grab me.

I stuffed the purse under my jacket and ran as fast as I could. I ran for a couple of blocks. By then I was out of breath. I slowed to a walk and tried to look normal, even though my heart was pounding in my chest.

I thought about throwing the purse away again—it was useless without the watch—but I couldn't make myself do it. I shoved it into my backpack.

I didn't go home straight away. Instead I went to Drew's place. I was soaking wet by the time I got there. I guess I must have smelled too, because when Drew answered the door, he wrinkled his nose and said, "Did you fall into a sewer on your way here?"

"I went back to that Dumpster to look for the purse."

That surprised him. He came out on the porch and closed the door behind him. "What did you do that for?"

I told him what Jana had told me.

"I wanted to find the watch," I said. "But it wasn't there. Someone must have taken it."

Drew looked away quickly, which made me think that something was wrong.

"Do you know where it is?" I asked.

He squirmed. "What would I want with an old watch?"

"What did you do with it, Drew?"

"What difference does it make? You can't give it to her. She'd know you were the one who took her grandma's purse."

"Where is it?"

"Forget about it, Kaz. It's gone."

"What do you mean, gone?"

He squirmed some more.

"I sold it."

"Sold it? You sold a broken-down old watch?"

"It may be broken, but I saw right away it was from World War Two. There's this store down on Gerrard Street that sells old war stuff. I sold it to the guy who runs the place. I was going to tell you, Kaz. Honest."

He should have told me in the alley when he first saw the watch. For sure he should have told me before he sold it. But none of that mattered now. All I cared about was what Jana had told me.

"I have to get that watch back," I said. "You have to give me the money you got for it."

"Aw, come on, Kaz—"

"This is important, Drew."

I could see he wanted to say no. But in the end, he dug in his pocket and handed over some money. I counted it. Then, in case I had made a mistake, I counted it again.

"He paid you *this* much for a watch that doesn't even work?" I said.

"He paid me more, but I spent some of it." I couldn't believe it. "I told you, Kaz," he said. "It's from World War Two. People collect stuff like that."

"Tell me again where the store is."

My next stop was the store on Gerrard Street where Drew had sold the watch. The place was small and crammed full of all kinds of war stuff—uniforms, medals, flags, badges, knives, you name it. I looked around. I peered into every display case. But I didn't see the watch.

"Can I help you with something?" the man behind the counter finally asked.

I told him what I was looking for and described it to him as best as I could remember.

The man shook his head.

"I don't have anything like that," he said.

"Yes, you do. My friend sold it to you."

We stared at each other for a few moments. Finally he reached down and opened a drawer under the counter. He pulled out the watch.

"That's it," I said. I took out the money Drew had given me and I handed it to the man.

The man counted it.

"That's not enough," he said.

"It's what you paid for it."

"It's what your friend sold it for. Now the watch belongs to me. I can sell it for five times as much. In fact, I know someone who'll pay me even more than that." He told me how much he was asking for the watch.

I just stared at him. I didn't have that much money. Finally I said the only thing I could think of: "That watch is stolen. I can call the police."

The man crossed his arms over his chest.

"You do that," he said. "And I'll tell the police about you and your friend. I'm sure they'll want to know how your friend got hold of a stolen watch and why you came in here and tried to buy it even though you know it's stolen. Hey, you know what?

Maybe I'll be a good citizen and *I'll* call them."

I felt like smashing one of the store's display cases. No matter what I did, things went wrong.

"Keep the stupid watch," I said. "I don't care."

The man didn't say anything. I sure hoped he wouldn't call the cops on me.

chapter ten

My mom was in the kitchen when I got home. "Kaz?" she called when she heard me come through the front door.

I hurried up to my room and stashed the purse in my closet.

"Kaz?" My mom appeared in the door to my room. "You're soaking wet," she said, looking from me to the wet spots on the carpet.

"I—I took a walk, and it started to rain."

"I can see that," she said. "Neil told me

you weren't here when he got home. I was getting worried."

"I'm sorry. It's just that—" I thought about the purse. My mom was looking at me, waiting for me to say something. "I hate school. I'm tired of being the dumbest kid there."

"You're not dumb," my mom said. "You have a disability. Lots of really smart people have the same disability."

"Tell that to Rufus."

"Who's Rufus?"

"He's the guy who picks on me all the time. That's why I got into trouble the other day. He never lets up."

She frowned. "Is this boy Rufus bullying you?"

"He's always making fun of me. And he's got lots of friends. They all back him up."

"Do you want me to talk to Ms. Everett?"

I shook my head. That would only make things worse.

"Maybe we can talk about how you can handle the situation," my mom said.

I didn't see what good that would do.

"We can role-play," she said. "There's a solution to every problem, Kaz. We can deal with this. You'll see." She gave me a hug. When she pulled back, her nose was wrinkled up. "Why don't you take a quick shower, put on some clean clothes and come downstairs," she said. "I have a surprise for you."

A surprise?

I showered and changed. My mom was waiting for me in the living room. There was a package sitting on the coffee table. It was wrapped in paper that had balloons all over it.

"Go ahead. Open it," she said.

I ripped the paper off. It was the games system I had wanted for my birthday. I stared at her.

"I guess hockey equipment wasn't such a good idea. We just thought that if you started to play again—" She shook her head. "Neil and I know you've been having a hard time, Kaz. We want you to be happy. We really do."

I looked at the games system again. "What about the hockey equipment?" I said. "Wasn't it expensive?"

"I returned it." She smiled at me. "Neil is out with some friends tonight, so it's just you and me. How about if I order a pizza, and you run down to the video store and rent a movie for us to watch?"

"Really?" My mom and I used to have movie nights at least once a week before Neil moved in. We hadn't had one in a long time.

"Really," my mom said. "In fact, get two movies. We'll make it a double feature. And don't forget the popcorn. We're going to celebrate."

"My birthday, you mean?"

She nodded. "And something else too." She was still smiling, but she looked a little nervous now. "Neil asked me to marry him."

What?

I stared at the games system.

"Is that why you and Neil bought me that?" I said. "As a bribe?"

"A bribe? What do you mean, Kaz?"

"I hate Neil. I hate that he lives here.

You could buy me a million presents and I'd still hate him."

"Kaz, please—"

I swept the box with the games system in it off the table. For a moment my mom did nothing. Then, slowly, she picked it up and put it back on the table.

"Neil is a good person, Kaz. I don't know how I would have got through the last couple of years without him."

"You said yes, didn't you?"

"I know the two of you will get along once you know each other better. You'll see."

"I'll never get along with him," I told her. "I want to live with Dad."

"Kaz—"

I went up to my room and slammed the door. I stayed there all night. Nothing was going right.

Nothing.

The games system was sitting on my desk when I woke up the next morning. My mom must have put it there after I fell asleep. Well, it could sit there forever as far as I was concerned. I didn't want it anymore.

"Hey, good morning, Sport," Neil said, grinning, the next morning when I went down to get something to eat. Did he think a games system was going to make me like him? Did he think I'd be so grateful that I would accept him as my new dad? I poured myself some cereal and took it up to my room to eat. I stared at the stupid games system while I chewed. I had practically begged for it, and now all I wanted to do was throw it out the window. I even thought about doing it. I thought about the crashing sound it would make when it hit the patio and the look Neil would have on his face when he yelled at me and told me how ungrateful I was. I stared at the stupid box.

My mom and Neil went grocery shopping after breakfast. While they were out, I called Drew. I needed his help with something—actually, with a couple of things.

"Can I sleep over at Drew's place tonight?" I asked my mom when she and Neil got back with the groceries.

"What about your homework?" Neil said.

"I'll do it tomorrow."

"Did Drew's mom say it was okay?" my mom asked.

"You can call her and double check," I said.

My mom frowned at me for a moment, like she was worried about something. Then she hugged me.

"Okay," she said. "But don't forget your toothbrush. And use it, Kaz, okay?"

I took my toothbrush and some clothes. I also took the purse. I didn't want my mom to find it while I was gone. I was going to throw it away again. And I took the games system. My mom smiled when she saw the box tucked under my arm.

"I hope you and Drew have a good time with that," she said. "But don't stay up all night, okay?"

chapter eleven

Drew and I went up to the mall. After we did what we had come for, we stopped by the food court for some Cokes. We were on our way to the bus stop when I heard someone call my name. It was Jana. She came over to Drew and me.

"I thought that was you," she said.

"Hey, Jana," I said. I wished she hadn't spotted me. I wished she would go away.

"I saw my grandma last night, and guess what?" she said. "She's going to be okay.

They're letting her go home on Monday." She sounded relieved about that. She smiled at me like she thought I should be happy for her.

"That's great," I said.

"Yeah, it really is."

She kept smiling at me.

"Did your dad tell her about the watch?" I asked finally.

Jana nodded. "My grandma was really upset. She cried. I've never seen her cry before. It made me want to cry too. But she talked to the police. She remembered a few things about the boys who stole her purse."

My heart slammed to a stop in my chest. Jana's grandmother had looked right at me. I wondered if she'd seen the scars under my hoodie.

"She wears glasses, and they fell off," she said. "But she saw one of the boys before the attack and she said she was pretty sure she would recognize him again if she saw him. And she said the other one was wearing a baseball cap." She glanced at Drew. He had on his baseball cap, just like always. "They were playing with a Frisbee. It's not much, but the police were really nice to her. They said they'd do their best."

"That's great," I said again.

Drew nudged me. "We have to get going, Kaz."

"Like I said, the police were really nice," Jana said. "They told my dad that they don't have a lot of time to go looking for purse snatchers, but they circulated a description of the watch and they put a notice out to all the pawnshops in case someone tries to pawn it. I guess that's something."

"I guess," I said.

Drew nudged me again.

"Anyway, I just wanted to tell you what's happening," Jana said. "You've been so nice about everything. I thought you'd like to know."

"Yeah," I said. My cheeks felt like they were on fire. "Thanks."

I said good-bye to Jana, and Drew and I practically ran to the bus. We found seats, and Drew punched me on the arm.

"I think The Princess has the hots for you," he said.

"She does not," I said. Then I couldn't help it: "You think so?"

"Definitely." Drew grinned. "Too bad it's too late, huh?"

I looked out the bus window. Jana hadn't turned out to be anything like I'd expected. She was nice to me. She didn't stare at my scars. She didn't say anything that made me feel stupid. She treated me like I was a regular guy. She had even offered to help me with my schoolwork.

Yeah, it was too bad it was too late.

A little later, Drew and I were standing outside the bus terminal downtown.

"So, I guess this is it," Drew said.

"Yeah."

"If your mom calls, I'll tell her you're in the bathroom or something."

"She won't call," I said. I'd slept over at Drew's house plenty of times. My mom had never called even once. She knew Drew's mom, so she never worried.

"She'll call eventually," Drew said.

"She'll call when you don't go home tomorrow."

"Then you can tell her the truth," I said. "It'll be too late for her to do anything about it."

Drew nodded. He looked at me and then down at the pavement. He shuffled his feet. "I guess I'm going to miss you," he said finally.

"I know I'm going to miss you," I said. Drew was the best friend I'd ever had. What if I never made another friend as good?

"Well, good luck," he said. "Call me when you get there, okay?"

I promised I would.

I watched Drew walk away. Then I pushed open the door to the bus station. There was a counter along one wall where you could buy tickets. I fished out the piece of paper where Drew had written down my dad's address and phone number, and I got into line. My stomach was doing back flips. I couldn't believe that I was actually here. My hand closed around the wad of bills that I had got when I returned the game system. I had been worried that it wasn't enough, so Drew called the bus station for me to check how much a one-way ticket would cost.

"You're golden," he said. "With the money from the watch and the money from the games system, you can buy a bus ticket and get something to eat whenever the bus pulls over for a rest stop, and you'll still have a little left over for when you get there."

The line moved forward.

I glanced around the bus station. It was full of people walking around, sitting and waiting for buses, reading, eating, drinking coffee. I wondered where they were all going. I wondered if any of them was as nervous as I was. It had been a long time since I'd seen my dad. My plan was to surprise him. I wondered what he would say when I finally got there and called to ask him to pick me up. I wondered what his new wife was like and whether his baby—a little girl, my half-sister—would like me. I wondered what school would be like where my dad lived.

The line moved forward again.

I thought about Drew and how he never made fun of me and never stared at my scars, and how he helped me with my homework as much as he could. I thought about Jana too. It was just my luck to meet someone as nice as her in such a stupid way. I wondered what she would think if she ever found out what I had done. I thought about her grandmother and her purse, which was still in my backpack. I felt sick when I thought about the watch. It had taken more than sixty years for that watch to make its way back to Jana's grandma. And then I had taken it.

"Next," a voice called. It was a ticket agent. He was looking right at me.

chapter twelve

Drew almost fell over when I surprised him at his locker on Monday morning.

"I thought you'd be at your dad's by now," he said. "What happened? Did your mom...?" He stopped and looked at me for a moment. "She never called our house," he said. "I was sure she would, but she never did. You...?"

"I changed my mind," I said.

"But you said you couldn't stand being around Neil anymore. You said—"

"Well, if you really want me to go—"

"No way," he said, grinning at me. He punched me on the arm. "Hey, you want to go up to the mall after school? You could buy that games system back..."

"No, I can't," I said. "I don't have enough money."

I had finally made it to the front of the line at the bus station when the ticket agent called out, "Next!" I started toward the counter. I was almost there when my feet stopped walking. The ticket agent looked impatiently at me. I looked down at the money in my hand. Then I turned and walked out of the bus station.

The man in the military antiques store scowled when he saw me, but it didn't take long before he changed his expression. From there I went to a postal outlet where I bought a big padded envelope. I filled it and sealed it and went up to the counter. I was relieved that I was the only person there besides the guy behind the counter. He looked at me, waiting for me to tell him what I wanted. I sucked in a deep breath and tried not to look as embarrassed as I felt. My mom always said that I should never feel embarrassed.

"I have a learning disability and I need help finding an address," I told the guy behind the counter. He was young, and I thought he was going to give me attitude. But he didn't. Instead he said, "Do you know the person's name?"

"The last name is King," I said.

He did something on his computer. "Do you have a first name or initial?" he said.

I knew Jana's name, but I didn't know her grandma's name. I shook my head.

"You know the street they live on?"

I knew the neighborhood—it was over near where Drew's mom worked. But I had no idea what street Jana's grandma lived on. I shook my head again.

The clerk sighed. "There are a lot of Kings in the city," he said. "If you want your package to get to the right one, I'm going to need either a first name or a street name."

Then I had an idea.

"Royal Avenue," I said.

He stared at me. "You're kidding, right? King on Royal Avenue?"

"I'm serious," I said.

He turned back to his computer screen. After a minute, his face changed. "Here it is," he said, sounding amazed. "D. King on Royal Avenue." He laughed. "You want me to write down the address for you?"

"Could you write it on the envelope?" I said. "My handwriting isn't very good."

He hesitated, but he did it, still without giving me any attitude.

"Do you want to put a return address on it?" he asked.

I shook my head and paid for the postage.

For the first time in a long time, I felt good about something I had done.

After I left the postal outlet, I made a phone call. It didn't go well. The good feeling I'd had when I arrived at the bus station had disappeared. I headed home.

"I thought you were sleeping over at Drew's tonight," my mom said when she saw me.

"Drew's brother is sick, so we had to cancel."

My mom studied my face for a few moments. "You don't look so well yourself," she said. She pressed a hand against my forehead. "Are you feeling okay, Kaz?"

"I'm going to go and lie down for a while," I said.

My mom nodded. "I'll check in on you later."

Jana came up to me at my locker two days later.

"Hey, Kaz," she said. "I wanted to tell you—my grandma got her watch back."

"She did?" I said, like it was a big surprise.

"She got her purse back too."

"Wow, that's great," I said. "She must be happy."

"She was thrilled. The very first thing she did was get my dad to take the watch to a repair place to see if they could get it running again. Then she's going to pack it up and send it to my brother in Afghanistan before anything else happens to it."

"I'm glad it worked out," I said. I was supposed to meet Drew in the cafeteria, but now I didn't want to go. I wanted to stay and talk to Jana. I wanted her to want to stay and talk to me.

"But it's weird," she said.

"What is?"

"Whoever had the purse sent it to my house instead of to my grandmother's place."

"Yeah? So?"

"You know what that means, don't you, Kaz?"

"No." I had no idea what she was getting at.

"Think about it," she said. "Whoever had the purse or whoever found it mailed it to my house. *My* house, Kaz."

All of a sudden I wished I was safe in the cafeteria with Drew—or that Drew was here with me so that he could help me figure out what was going on and what to say.

"Maybe they didn't know where your grandma lived," I said.

"That's the thing," Jana said.

What was the thing? What was she talking about?

"All the ID was gone out of my grandma's purse," Jana said. "So, either it fell out or the person who stole the purse got rid of it."

"There you go," I said. "Whoever returned the purse probably didn't know where she lived."

"Exactly!" Jana said. "And you know what *that* means, don't you?"

I glanced around. Maybe Drew had got tired of waiting for me. Maybe he would come and look for me.

"It means that whoever returned the purse has to be someone who knows me," Jana said.

What?

"How do you figure that?"

"My grandma got married again after my grandpa died. She doesn't have the same last name as my dad. So how would anyone know to send her purse to our house unless they heard me talking about what happened?"

"Someone else in your family must have talked about it," I said.

"Maybe," Jana said. She didn't sound convinced. "But it was a kid who knocked her over. And she told the police that he said he was sorry. She said he asked if she was okay."

I started to get a bad feeling.

"I have to go, Jana," I said. "I'm supposed to meet Drew."

I started to walk away from her. She followed me.

"She said the boy who knocked her down was wearing a sweatshirt with the hood pulled up. She said she's not sure, but before she got knocked down, she thinks she saw a scar on the side of his face."

I wanted to run away. I didn't know what to say.

"Anyway," she said, "I just wanted to tell you that she got her stuff back and that she's really happy about the watch. I thought you'd want to know—you know, because you asked me about it and you seemed to care."

I waited for her to say more, but she didn't. She just turned and walked away.

When I got home and saw that my mom was there, I was sure that Jana had called the cops.

"How come you're home so early?" I said.

"We have to talk, Kaz."

Uh-oh. My legs started to shake. My face got all red.

"Mom, I'm sorry. I didn't—"

"Your dad called me at work today."

That wasn't what I had expected at all. I was relieved—until I took a second look at the expression on her face. She was really upset.

"He says you called him on Saturday, Kaz."

It was true. I had phoned my dad right after I left the postal outlet. I still wanted to go and stay with him, but I had used up most of my money to buy back Jana's grandma's watch. I didn't have enough left to pay for a bus ticket.

"He said that you asked him to send you bus fare so that you could go out there and live with him. He said—" Her eyes got all watery. "He said he hung up on you."

I don't know what surprised me more—that my dad had hung up on me or that he had called my mom and told her about it.

"Is that true?" my mom said.

I nodded. I didn't tell her that after he hung up, I called him again, but he didn't answer the phone.

"How did you even find out how to get in touch with him?" she said.

"Drew helped me."

My mom sighed. "Sit down," she said.

I sank down onto the couch. She sat down next to me and held one of my hands.

"It's my fault," she said.

What was her fault?

"What do you mean, Mom?"

"I mean..." She peered into my eyes. "I thought that it would be easier for you if you thought that I didn't want you to be with your dad, if you thought I wanted you all to myself. Do you understand what I'm saying, Kaz?"

I had already figured it out. I mean, what kind of dad hangs up on his own kid and then doesn't even answer when his kid calls back?

"Is it because I'm so dumb?" I said. "Is that why he doesn't want me around?"

"No," my mom said. "It has nothing to do with that. And you are *not* dumb."

"Then why did he hang up on me?"

My mom squeezed my hand.

"Your father had a hard time dealing with what happened, with the fire," she said at last.

She had to be kidding. *He* had a hard time dealing with the fire? What about me? I was the one who had been in the hospital forever. I was the one who had to have those skin grafts. I was the one with the horrible scars that everyone stared at. What could *he* possibly have had a hard time dealing with?

"I saved his life," I said. My dad had fallen asleep on the couch with a lit cigarette in his hand. I'd been asleep, but something woke me up. Then I smelled smoke. I ran out of the house, just like my mom had told me I should do if there was a fire. I screamed for my dad, but he didn't come out. So I ran back into the house to find him. "If I hadn't woken up when I did, he would have died."

"Kaz," my mom said gently, "if you hadn't woken up when you did, *you* would have died too." I stared at her. I had never thought about that before, and she had never said it to me. I wondered if she had said it to my dad. I wonder if that's what they had fought about.

"Your father blames himself for what happened to you. I think when he looks at you, it makes him remember what he did. I think he'd rather forget. I think—" She stopped suddenly. "I'm sorry, Kaz."

I felt numb all over. I didn't know what to say.

"I love you, Kaz," she said. "No matter what. I love you and I want you to stay here with me—and Neil. I don't know what I would do without you."

She started to cry. I hugged her to try to get her to stop. Then I said something that was guaranteed to make her start all over again.

"Mom," I said. "There's something I have to tell you."

chapter thirteen

Two Saturdays later, I was standing on a chair in Jana's grandma's kitchen, handing dishes down to Drew. He was stacking them on the counter. After we emptied the cupboards, we were going to wash the shelves and put down new shelf paper. Then we had to put everything back. Drew wasn't too happy about it, but I didn't mind. In fact, I was glad to be doing it.

Jana's grandma was sitting at the kitchen table watching us. She was telling us about

Jana's grandfather, who had died when Jana's father was in high school. She was friendly and smiled a lot, which wasn't at all what I had expected. I'd been terrified to ring her buzzer. Even Drew was scared, and he always acted like nothing could ever get to him. We were sure she was going to call the cops on us. But she didn't. Instead she asked me and Drew and our moms to come in, and she made us tea. My mom was as nervous as I was, but it worked out okay. Jana's grandma said that she was glad I'd returned her watch and her purse and that we could make up for everything else by doing some chores for her. I agreed for both of us before Drew could say anything.

It turned out that I liked her. I liked listening to her talk about her brother and what it had been like reading all about the war in his letters and wondering all the time if he was okay. I also liked listening to her talk about what it had been like when she was raising Jana's dad. Things sure had been different then.

We finished washing all the cupboards. I put in the shelf paper, just like Jana's grandma showed me. Then we started putting the dishes away. We had just finished when the doorbell rang. Jana's grandma excused herself and went to answer it. I heard Jana's voice. I wished I could hide. I hadn't talked to Jana since that day in school.

She came into the kitchen with her grandma. She said, "I heard you were here," and she didn't even sound mad.

"I was just going to offer the boys some tea and cookies," Jana's grandma said. "Would you like to join us?"

"Sure," Jana said. She pulled a little box from her pocket. "Dad picked this up today," she said. "He asked me to give it to you."

Jana's grandma gasped when she opened the little box. There was a watch inside, but it wasn't rusty anymore. It was bright and silvery, and I could see the second hand moving. She lifted the watch out of the box and turned it over. There were tears in her eyes when she read the name and the identification number engraved on the back.

"I'll pack it up and send it to your brother first thing on Monday," she said. She reached out and squeezed my hand. "Thank you, Kaz," she said.

I just stared at her. I had taken the watch from her in the first place and here she was thanking me. Even if I'd known what to say—which I didn't—I couldn't have spoken. There was a big lump in my throat.

Jana's grandma smiled at me. "There are some cookies in that tin over there, Jana," she said. "Would you put some on a plate while I start the kettle boiling? You boys sit down. You've done enough for one day."

I sat down next to Drew and watched Jana's grandma bustle around her kitchen. She wasn't at all what I'd thought when I first saw her. I hoped she felt the same way about me. I looked down at the watch in that little box and was glad for at least part of what I'd done.

Author's Note

In November, 1990, a hunter came across the wreckage of an airplane in a remote area in Burma (also known as Myanmar). Among the wreckage, he found a watch that was inscribed with the name and service number of Flying Officer William Kyle. William Kyle had been a crew member on a plane that had disappeared in June, 1945. The hunter gave the watch to a missionary, who realized that it had belonged to a serviceman. Five years later, the watch made its ways to Veterans Affairs Canada, which returned it to William Kyle's family. In 1996, the bodies of William Kyle and his crew members were recovered and given a proper burial. To the best of my knowledge, the watch was never stolen from William Kyle's family.

Norah McClintock is a five-time winner of the Arthur Ellis Award for Best Juvenile Crime Novel. Norah lives in Toronto, Ontario.

Orca Currents

Visit www.orcabook.com for all Orca titles.

Orca Currents

Visit www.orcabook.com for all Orca titles.

Orca Currents

Visit www.orcabook.com for all Orca titles.